Try Something New

An Ivy and Mack story

Written by Juliet Clare Bell

Illustrated by Gustavo Mazali

Collins

Aunt Libby

Ivy

Mina

🎧 On Friday afternoon, Mr Hill said to Ivy's class, "It's fun to try different things. This weekend, let's all try something new!"

4

Ivy said, "Something new? I haven't got any ideas. Have you, Mina?"

Mina said, "Maddy's got new hair."

5

That evening, Ivy was in the kitchen with her family. She thought about her homework.

"Mum?" she said. "What new thing ..."

"Would you like a cheese and banana sandwich, Ivy?" asked Dad.

"No, thank you." said Ivy.

Ivy said, "Mum, I have homework. Can I go to the hairdresser, please?"

"Why? For homework?" asked Mum.

"Yes," said Ivy. "I want short hair."

Mum said, "Short hair? Let's talk in the morning."

"Short hair?" said Mack. "But I like your long hair, Ivy."

Dad said, "It's Ivy's hair. She can choose."

Aunt Libby said, "I can take you to the hairdresser."

"You're very quiet, Ivy," said Aunt Libby. "Are you Ok?"

The hairdresser said, "Hello. I'm Jane!"

Ivy and Aunt Libby looked at some photos. "I like this one," said Aunt Libby. "Oh, I love this one. And this one! What do you think, Ivy?"

BEFORE

AFTER

Ivy and Aunt Libby sat down in front of the mirrors.

Jane, the hairdresser, picked up the scissors ...

"Be careful with your new hair!" said Jane.

Ivy said, "That was fun."

Aunt Libby said, "Yes, it was."

Aunt Libby asked, "Well ... do you like it?"

"Yes, I do!" said Ivy.

"Is it very short?" asked Dad.

"Yes," said Aunt Libby.

Ivy said, "But it looks very nice!"

Mack said, "Let me see!"

Ivy showed them her hair.

Mack said, "I don't understand.
That's not short!"

Ivy said, "No, *this* isn't short.
But THAT is!

Everyone looked at Aunt Libby's new
short hair.

Wow!
It's great!

18

"I wanted to try something new," said Ivy. "But I *like* my long hair."

Aunt Libby said, "And I wanted short hair!"

It's fantastic, Libby!

Ivy said, "Mum, what about my homework? Mr Hill said 'Try something new this weekend'."

Then Ivy had an idea.

"Dad?" she said. "Can I try one of your cheese and banana sandwiches, please?"

Picture dictionary

Listen and repeat

long

short

hair

hairdresser

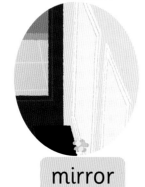

mirror

scissors

1 Look and order the story

2 Listen and say

Collins

Published by Collins
An imprint of HarperCollins*Publishers*
Westerhill Road
Bishopbriggs
Glasgow
G64 2QT

HarperCollins*Publishers*
1st Floor, Watermarque Building
Ringsend Road
Dublin 4
Ireland

William Collins' dream of knowledge for all began with the publication of his first book in 1819.

A self-educated mill worker, he not only enriched millions of lives, but also founded a flourishing publishing house. Today, staying true to this spirit, Collins books are packed with inspiration, innovation and practical expertise. They place you at the centre of a world of possibility and give you exactly what you need to explore it.

10 9 8 7 6 5 4 3 2

ISBN 978-0-00-839833-0

Collins® and COBUILD® are registered trademarks of HarperCollins*Publishers* Limited

www.collins.co.uk/elt

British Library Cataloguing in Publication Data

A catalogue record for this publication is available from the British Library.

Author: Juliet Clare Bell
Illustrator: Gustavo Mazali (Beehive)
Series editor: Rebecca Adlard
Publishing manager: Lisa Todd
Product managers: Jennifer Hall and Caroline Green
In-house editor: Alma Puts Keren
Project manager: Emily Hooton
Editor: Deborah Friedland
Proofreaders: Natalie Murray and Michael Lamb
Cover designer: Kevin Robbins
Typesetter: 2Hoots Publishing Services Ltd
Audio produced by id audio, London
Reading guide author: Julie Penn
Production controller: Rachel Weaver
Printed and bound by: GPS Group, Slovenia

MIX
Paper from
responsible sources
FSC™ C007454

Download the audio for this book and a reading guide for parents and teachers at www.collins.co.uk/839833